THE RULES OF LIFE

The Harper Short Novel Series

FAY WELDON

THE RULES OF LIFE

ILLUSTRATIONS BY AMANDA FAULKNER

Harper & Row, Publishers, *New York*
Cambridge, Philadelphia, San Francisco
London, Mexico City, São Paulo, Singapore, Sydney

A hardcover edition of this book was published in 1987 by Harper &
Row, Publishers.

First PERENNIAL LIBRARY edition published 1988.

DESIGNED BY LYDIA LINK

Library of Congress Cataloging-in-Publication Data

Weldon, Fay.
    The rules of life.

    (The Harper short novel series)
    "Perennial Library."
    I. Title.
    PR6073.E374R8   1988   823'.914   86-46107
ISBN 0-06-091499-0 (pbk.)

88 89 90 91 92 FG 10 9 8 7 6 5 4 3 2 1

THE RULES OF LIFE

STRANGE DAYS INDEED! Your narrator, in the year 2004, sits and works at his console within the great portals of the Temple that was once the British Museum, and tries to come to terms with the world, and his life, and the past. Envisage me, if you can, dressed in the white samite, mystic, wonderful, which is worn by the pulp priests of the GNFR, or Great New Fictional Religion: a small elderly male figure, dwarfed by rows upon ranks of the flickering electronic devices which these days bring the voices of the dead to life.

The pinner priests, our seniors in the GNFR hierarchy, also wear white samite but theirs is shot with multicoloured phosphorescent thread, the better to impress the not easily impressed. A strange sight indeed, as they crouch by night in every graveyard in the land, their Sony sensors at the ready, pinning down the ghostly emanations of the dear and not so dear departed — or re-winds as they have come to be called.

I am not as young as I was. I ought by now, with the wisdom of the GNFR at my command, to have achieved contentment, to have learned to acquiesce in my fate, but as my fingers stray over the patterns made by this particular re-wind, they tremble. I am full of a longing which can never be satisfied — to touch what is untouchable, but only just; feel what can't be felt, but once almost was. The dead are more powerful than we suppose, than the pinner priests let on. We are expected to learn wisdom from the re-winds — but who ever learned wisdom from a ghost? Call them what you will, that is all they are.

The ghost of Gabriella Sumpter — for this was her name in life — is registering in an unusual fashion. She wishes, I gather, to discuss the rules of life, as seen from the vantage of hindsight, from a life which includes its death, and does not exclude it. Or so I must judge from the patterns emerging from the console. Here for the first time we have not merely scraps of memory, plus little wafts of resentment and spasms of desire, but some kind of search for understanding and completion. It hurts her: I can tell from her voice, and I don't want anyone hurt, not even a woman as selfish and morally frail as Gabriella Sumpter.

Well, he who pays the piper calls the tune, and the pinner priests do that, and the pulp priests must submit to their judgement, and to that of the Great Screen Writer In The Sky whose will we all serve, and whose priest — though a humble one — I am. Praise be the GSWITS: press Play and Record: consent!

Gabriella Sumpter first startled me by observing that there were no rules in fiction, and that if she wished to start with her death and end with her birth, she would. She could run life backwards if she wanted; yes, even that. I may say the voice was particularly attractive: light and low, and with just a hint of mirth and more than a hint of wilfulness. After death, voice-age goes back to a median point of about, I should say, thirty-three. Should the pinner priests ever manage a bodily resurrection, I daresay the same phenomenon would apply. Grandpa's re-wind would rise from his coffin in his vigorous prime. Not always a happy thought! But then – and this perhaps is the reason the GNFR is sweeping the Western World – we do acknowledge that the GSWITS has had many a bad idea in his time. Virtue lies in trying to make the best of His mistakes.

Now. Gabriella Sumpter went on to remark that although in fiction there were no rules, in life there were, and she, who had done so little good in her life except to herself, after her death would now like to help by passing a few on – or rather, back.

She had observed in life that the mass of ordinarily accepted rules – for example, that too many cooks spoil the broth, or if you can't stand the heat you should get out of the kitchen, or that a woman needs a man as a fish needs a bicycle, were simply not true: mere patterns of words, cement grouting for the shaky constructions of our existence, cosmetic rather than structural. But now she was dead, she had been able to come to a few, she felt, quite sound conclusions. Or Valid Rules, as she liked to call them.

'I have been dead for three months now,' she says, 'and the earth has settled sufficiently for a headstone to be placed on my grave. This is the first of the Valid Rules, an easy one: that headstones must wait for passions to ease; for grief and rage to abate. The earth sinks and settles with the emotions. My little ankle is devoid of flesh; my high round bosom quite de-natured; my soft eyes deliquesced and gone. They have written upon the slab *Gabriella Sumpter: 1941–2002. R.I.P.*'

Well might they inscribe 'R.I.P.'! How can anyone rest in peace now that the pinner priests lurk by night in every graveyard, with their re-play devices to the ground? I am surprised Gabriella had not asked for cremation, as so many

[13]

do these days. Not that burning the body destroys the recall voices: but it does at least scramble them to the point of indecipherability. Do we not have enough trouble with the living? Do we have to add the dead to our burdens? But there, the human quest for knowledge is as unrootupable as couch grass in a field. There is no stopping our pinner priests.

Miss Sumpter continues. 'Could they say of me that mine was a successful life? I think so. I did not marry; I did not have children. That was my great achievement. We cannot escape the destiny of being born — we *are*, therefore we must *be*, so the best we can do, while living, is not, by marrying, to burden others with our existence, and not, irresponsibly, by having children, to pass life on. Those are the second and third Rules. There is more than enough life about,' she says dismissively, 'and most of it is painful, and the briefer the experience the better.

'I consider myself fortunate,' she continues, 'to have died at 61, in full possession of my faculties, and still capable of inspiring erotic love, the only thing that makes life worth living at all. My step did not have time to falter, my spine did not curve; my eyes had wrinkled but barely dimmed: my teeth, with considerable help from my dentist, Edgar Simpson, remained white, firm, even, and above all *there*. Edgar Simpson, poor man, loved me quite desperately but I did not return his passion. I know, rationally, that dentists, like vets, are even more highly trained than are doctors, but, unlike doctors, they remain difficult to take seriously in the romantic sense. Theirs seems a primarily manual skill, and of a slightly absurd kind. Yet God knows we need them. *Nothing is fair* — that is the next of the Valid Rules: perhaps the greatest and most reliable of them all.'

Here Miss Sumpter goes on to complain about the smallness of the earth's circumference: a mere 24,000 miles. What kind of size is that, she demands, for a whirling stone globe to which so many million people are obliged to cling in their search for meaning. Unbelievably, immorally small! Yet still they insist, clinging head-down to the railway-track of life, listening to the approaching rumble of meaning: lifting their heads, crying 'it's coming, it's coming, the meaning is coming,' only it never quite does, of course. Some signal is against the train, its driver altogether too responsible, the train slows, stops, fades: death comes before enlightenment. (The dead do mix their metaphors: I am sorry. I think myself the re-recording procedures are more at fault than the re-winds — it doesn't seem too much to ask that some of the millions which pour daily into the GNFR coffers should go to refining the Technology of Truth. It is in its infancy, not its maturity as some seem to think.)

'I was buried in a white silk shift,' Miss Sumpter goes on, when the text has settled down again. 'I had it specially made by Frieda Martock: her poor old eyes were scarcely fit for the task. She had always been old, even when I was young, as the serving classes tend to be. It was the last thing she did for me. I insisted that she do it by hand: machine-stitching is far too brutal for fine silk; if the thread is strong enough to stand the mechanical pounding it will be strong enough to damage the fabric. Sewing thread must be no thicker than the thread of the stuff to which it is applied: the needle no coarser than its weave. Miss Martock's hands were painful and knotted by arthritis: it hurt them to wield the needle. But beauty is created by sacrifice, by pain and suffering. That is something else I have observed. Palaces built by enslaved and miserable serfs are more intricately beautiful, more reflective of human aspiration, than any number of concrete town halls built by well-fed enfranchised time-servers. If there is no sacrifice, the God does not descend. He likes blood. Miss Martock groaned while she worked, and so the shift hung beautifully. I rose from my death bed and tried it on once or twice before I died, and admired myself in it in the mirror, and almost sent a message to say how well she had done; but it does not do to praise too much. People get slack and stop bothering. That is another of the valid rules. Moreover, she had left a loose thread in one of the buttonholes.

'I died of cancer of the liver. It is not a painful death. One just gets more and more languid, and finally expires. I recommend it.

'The mirror in which I looked at myself, the better to study Miss Martock's silk shift, was old and gilt-framed, and the glass mercury-based. I do not like the new ground mirrors, which hate what they see and so distort the truth unpleasantly. I have, or had in my life, no particular appetite for truth: I think what has happened is that the sheer languor of my last living days prevented me from keeping it at bay. Much sheer effort goes into avoiding truth: left to itself, it sweeps in like the tide. This vision which I have, now I am dead, was not mine for most of my life. You now, you listeners to my soul, you pinner priests, have the benefit of my weariness.

'The house in which I had been living, in which I died, is not up for sale, since it is what's called a Grace and Favour residence – that is to say in the keeping of the Royal Family to dispose of as they want. Terra Rosa, 21 Marlborough Court, London, NW8, pink-washed, discreet, charming. I wonder who will have it next? Perhaps Timothy Tovey's eldest son James has a mistress, who could make use of it? I doubt it: he is altogether too boring, and genteel, as are all the children that my lover Timothy Tovey and his wife Janice made. Theirs was not a good mix, genetically. I told him it would be so, when the matter of his marrying Janice first arose: such a tall, pale, wavery woman! Perhaps Timothy Tovey's mother will have her way in the end, and move into Terra Rosa? She is nearing ninety now. Well, we will see. (The dead see everything. That is all the punishment they need.) But the house is so delightful! A small, pink and white detached double-fronted Georgian villa, with a balconied bedroom over the front door, where in summer breakfasting lovers can sip their morning coffee and not care who sees. Well, I never cared. Timothy Tovey of course did. Mistresses may be known to exist, but not seen publicly to exist. Either his mother Julia would get to hear of it, or his wife Janice, or the passing ambassador of some friendly (or unfriendly) nation catch a glimpse of him. Timothy is in the Diplomatic Service: he cannot afford scandal.

'Timothy Tovey was there at my bedside while I died. He left the palace reception where Janice was being awarded some medal or other for her perfectly boring work amongst the underprivileged and came at once. He had witnessed my face in that Little Death often enough: why not now in the great and final one? Poor Timothy: at thirty tall, vigorous and proud, a gorilla of a man, huge-headed, long-armed, with the bright, bright eyes of the very intelligent; and the slow drawl of the overcultivated: at seventy, stooped and haggard — a long time now since he broke every chair he sat upon, made me cry out in fear for the safety of my small bones as he gripped me in our love-making. The cheekbones were still firm and prominent but the flesh caved in greyly beneath them. The jaw still jutted in its obstinate way, but the skin folded unkindly below. (Oh, what age does to us! Listen, I am glad to be dead: hurry, hurry, everyone, to join me!) But still he had the same bleak, bright, sideways look of defiance: now directed at the death which was to divide us, as in the past it had been directed at wives, mothers, children, politicians, prime ministers, kings — everyone who stood between us. He held my hand as I died.

'Shall I tell you what happened at the moment of death?'

Here I maintain that the pinner priests have failed again. The version is garbled. My superiors maintain that the GSWITS, for his own purpose, does his best to keep this particular matter veiled. But the Great Scriptwriter has an editor himself, does he not, to whom, presumably, representation from we bit-part players in the great drama of the universe can be made? I do not believe that this is heresy: surely we, who have to put up with the pain and torments of the life he has decreed, have a human right to *know more*. If the GSWITS won't satisfy us, won't divulge the plot and purpose, surely those above Him will? The pinner priests say it is not our part so much as to conceive of the GSWITS himself as requiring guidance. But there are many others who think like me — who recognise a B-movie writer for what he is; more of us perhaps than the pinner priests realise.

Miss Sumpter described the moment of death in these terms. Her eyes misted; she was gazing at her hand, held in its turn by her lover's hand. As she looked, the finger shapes became vague, turned, twisted, entwined and stretched and grew into a handsome, leafless tree on which hung a single fruit — and it was she. The fruit dropped, into something soft, like meadow grass — she imagined that sensation of falling and of being received was the actual moment of death — and as it dropped everything changed; as in the cutting of a film one scene abruptly passes to the next. She was in a long, long corridor; reddish, warm — one wonders whether she describes the birth canal: the reverse journey which must happen, spiritually, as we retreat from life? — and along this corridor she travelled, swiftly and composedly, and with great joy, knowing it was back the way she had come. And, as she passed, person after person stepped from the doors which lined the corridor — friends, some she knew and recognised, others she had forgotten but now remembered. They greeted her, welcomed her, fell in with her — though it no longer seemed her corporeal self, but spirit, soul, which swept along — so that when she reached the end of the endless corridor — it seems all things are possible after death — and stepped out into a great white brilliant space she was, as it were, the concentration of everything she had ever known, everyone she had ever greeted, the sum of every flush of excitement, every effort at communication, every animation she had ever experienced — every emotion now showing its true and finer face; every insult and every humiliation now made good, repented of. It was as if, forgiving others in the sheer pleasure and excitement of their company, she needed no forgiveness herself — and she was in paradise, which was, simply, other people. What was more, it was not boring.

Well, so the pinner priests recorded Miss Sumpter's account of the experience of death. I must say, myself, that if she is telling the truth, and they have recorded it accurately, she has got off very lightly, considering her behaviour in life.

Of course we in the GNFR do try to avoid the condemnation of others but sometimes it's hard. Though virtue lies in consenting to the parts allotted to us, and we recognise that, just as some can't help being victims others can't help being oppressors, and that the best we can do is help the Great Plot of Life go forward, with all its myriad, myriad sub-plots, sometimes we can't help shaking our heads in disapproval. Part of me, the unreformed part, still sees Gabriella Sumpter as an adulteress, a woman too selfish, too self-centred to have children, who did nothing useful in all her life, for anyone. Yet, in the terms of the GNFR, she is a saint. She did not stand in the way of events. She went where the script dictated — where Fate led her. The fault must surely be in my comprehension, not in the manner of her living. Bow the head! Assent!

I try, but the thought will not be kept down — perhaps the GNFR *is* in error. Perhaps, in this world of initials we seem increasingly obliged to inhabit, as the pace of living hots up, as the GSWITS covers more and more pages, yet another initial is needed? The GNFR must become the RGNFR, the Revised Great New Fictional Religion. Am I perhaps the one to bring it about — not too humble, nor too elderly, after all? Gabriella Sumpter has stirred something in me I thought was dead. Oh, all our prayers must go to ensuring happy endings! Let us simply accept that the GSWITS allocated to us mortals is a mere B-feature writer, with the unhappy tendency of his kind to introduce disasters — cyclones, volcanic eruptions, earthquakes or man-made explosions — to get himself out of plot difficulties. The effort of His creation must therefore be to see that He takes his task seriously, and improves his standards. I will not have it that this is heresy. One day we will come to recognise it — when we have had our fill of Watergates, plummetting Jumbos, Titanics raised, AIDS, Chernobyls — then at last the human race will properly grasp that it is not even a main feature, but some kind of hotch-potch of a supporting fictional exercise. We will be happier when we can accept it. We will have fewer expectations. And I think that then, when the RGNFR is triumphant, when the new race of pinner priests — of which I will be lord — recall the likes of Gabriella Sumpter, it will be with the whiff of sulphur, not the taste of ambrosia. I want her punished. There must be punishment.

Well! Miss Sumpter went on to talk of laundry. In fact at times she seemed more concerned with the rules of laundry than the rules of life.

'One of my earliest memories', says Miss Sumpter, 'was of attending a children's mass in a crisp white cotton dress trimmed with blue velvet braid. My mother, Emerald Lacey-Sumpter, took great care to see that I was always prettily and appropriately dressed, or rather saw to it that Nanny McGorrah accomplished the task. I must have been five. The sermon was given by Father McCree, a priest with little piggy eyes and a soft mouth. He told us a story of the great and wonderful party which was being given up at the castle, to which all the children, rich and poor, had been invited. (The only condition of entrance was that the child had to arrive at the front door clothed in spotless white.) And how one little girl, properly dressed and on her way to the party, stopped at a bush full of dark-red, luscious blackberries, and was tempted, and pulled a single branch down and carefully, carefully picked one, believing she could eat and not get dirty. But as she let go the branch a cluster of berries brushed the front of

her dress and stained it purple, red and black! There was no getting those stains out! The little girl stopped by a brook and did her best, but though the sparkling water ran for a while blood-red, her dress was even messier than before. Weeping and disgraced, and trailing behind the joyous, spotless throng, the poor child stood at the palace gates begging to be let in, but the gatekeeper, sadly and gravely, shook his head and the gate was shut in her face. All the other children went in to endless bliss. Not she!

'Do not, I beg you, said Father McCree, at the children's service, be like the little girl who in her wilfulness stained her purity. How I hated the priest with his little piggy eyes and his soft mouth; he'd never tasted a big ripe luscious blackberry in all his life. I knew it intuitively, even as I knew his fat white hand, if only it dared, would creep up under my crisp blue-braided cotton dress, and stretch the gap between my pale pink knickers, and in and up to peek and pry, as if the nails of his fingers were eyes and could see.

'When I got home I spilled ink all over my dress. I wanted to be stained. Nanny McGorrah did her best to get the splodges out, but used hot water instead of cold, thus fixing the stain. Ink-spots should be removed by dipping the part first into cold water, and only then into hot, then spreading the fabric on the hand or the back of a spoon, pouring a few drops of oxalic acid or salts of sorrel over the stain, and rubbing and rinsing in cold water until removed. Alas, my mother, Lady Emerald, was no more knowledgeable than Nanny McGorrah in such matters; all their efforts achieved was the spreading and splodging of the stains, and the dress had to be abandoned altogether. A pity. My mother could never keep her mind on anything difficult or unpleasant for more than five minutes at a time. My father was consistently unfaithful to her, knowing it scarcely mattered. A new hat or an outing to a tea-dance would quickly cure any sense of grievance she might have. I think they were very, very happy together. I was their only child. I took care to be pleasant and loving towards them, whilst reserving kicking, biting, spitting and shouting for Nanny McGorrah, who loved me in spite of it. I remember concluding at an early age that she was obliged to love me, inasmuch as I was her source of income.

'People love where it is in their interests to love,' remarked Miss Sumpter, 'that is another observable rule of life. Love is the great excuse: *I cannot leave my wife because I love her* means, "I cannot leave my wife because of the inconvenience and trouble involved, and besides I am frightened." *I will not leave this nannying job because I love the child* merely means, "the devil I know is better than the devil I don't." Nanny McGorrah was a weak, sloppy, amiable and sentimental woman. Her stomach – she undressed in front of me thinking, wrongly, that my childish eyes were uncritical – hung in folds over white flannelette drawers. I resolved I would never allow my stomach to do such a thing. My father's belly stuck out proudly: it went before him as a token of his amiability, prowess and success. Timothy Tovey's, I may say, did the same for a year or so, when he was in his early fifties. Janice put him on a diet. (*Put him on a diet!* What impudence. How wives do delight in pretending to be mothers!)

'Timothy Tovey would come straight from some dinner party, where his wife had obliged him to dine on melon, lean steak and salad and black coffee, to the bedroom at Terra Rosa, where I would press cream chocolates between his lips with my tongue, to assuage his hunger. Or else we would simply go out to dine, publicly. Hunger, even more than lust, makes a man imprudent. Janice could not understand why he took so long to lose weight. Poor Timothy, married to such a fool! But, of course, a rich fool. We both benefited from Janice's wealth, and connections.

'I have never been an ostentatious spender: it is vulgar to be seen to spend. But it is undeniable that I have always liked to be surrounded by what is fine, and delicate, and subtle — and such things are not cheap. Our bedspread was of golden lace laid over black lace, laid over white: Frieda Martock would come in once every three months to see to its cleaning. The three layers would first be unpicked and separated. To clean the gold lace she would mix the crumb of a 2lb loaf with $\frac{1}{4}$lb of powder blue — still to be found in a few hardware shops. The crumb would be rubbed fine and the blue mixed with it, and the mixture simply laid plentifully on the lace, until it brightened. Then the lace would be brushed clean with flannel and rubbed up gently, very gently, with a piece of crimson velvet. The result never failed. The black lace would be passed through a warm liquor of water and bullock's gall (Harrods supplied this, for a large fee: I used Janice's name) then rinsed out in cold water. A small portion of glue would be dissolved in boiling water, and the lace passed through it; Miss Martock would clap the stuff here and there with her rheumy hands — clap, clap; the sound of *attention to detail* rang through that pretty proper little house, as it had for more than two hundred years — to revive and restore its texture, and then pin it in a special frame to dry.

'It was in fact the frame of one of the very large family paintings which my first suitor, the arsonist Walter James, had taken into his head to burn, hoping thus to avenge his wrongs. The frame had escaped the fire: it was the last thing my father managed to save before the fire consumed him too, and now it served this excellent purpose. That did for the black lace — the layer of white silk bone lace took longer than anything, of course. First Miss Martock had to unstitch the composing pieces — the spread was made of twenty sections, each nine inches wide. These she wound around some six specially prepared muslin-wrapped glass bottles, tacking lightly into place to prevent wrinkles, matching edge to edge exactly. Over these layers she would place a linen cloth, which she would rub firmly with soap and cold water, and leave overnight for the lather to seep through the layers. The whole would then be rinsed through and through with cold water — never hot, for hot water yellows any white fabric, and of course weakens it — preferably outside, but never in direct sunlight. The lace would next be unwrapped, laid flat to dry, restitched, the covering layers of black lace and then the gold sewn, and the whole placed back upon the bed. Sometimes Timothy Tovey and I made love upon the bedcover and not beneath it: gold lace is ever so slightly scratchy, and we liked that. I felt it was right that my skin should suffer, even as the lace did, and *vice versa* — that to contribute, even in a minor way, towards this pinnacle of human pleasure, the feel of his flesh in mine, mine around his, tongue to nipple, nipple to teeth, was worth a little damage to the lace! Even that we should, in the course of time, wear it altogether away seemed no bad thing.

I could feel, as my naked skin encountered the lace, the frisson of poor Frieda Martock's disapproval. She lived and will no doubt die (unless, poor old soul, she is raped by one of those city prowlers who have a penchant for old ladies) a virgin. The nearest she can get to the sacrament of sex is by the patient washing of the lace which covers my and Timothy Tovey's illicit bed. Frieda Martock was born patient, good and plain, not brilliant and bright, into a world which killed off the males of her generation by the million and doomed her kind to a dismal half-life. From them that hath not shall be taken away. That is the rule engraved in gold over the Gates of Life.

'Janice Tovey has easy-care sheets in polyester, and terylene-filled duvets, and Timothy told me once he and she had twin beds. Although when, some fifteen years ago, a series of television documentaries on the historic political houses of London was screened, and the cameras went inside the Tovey household, it seemed to me that their bed was very double indeed: or else – worse – that the beds had been pushed together. I had never myself been in their bedroom, although Timothy Tovey and I often enough made love in the spare room extension above the big garages where the Rolls and Bentleys were kept. He liked to have me on his premises: he would have had me in his and Janice's bedroom, but I always refused. So vulgar! As if we took the marriage seriously enough thus to insult it.

'The sight of the double bed did, I admit, disconcert me. I switched off the television set and waited for Timothy Tovey to come round at eleven for his chilled cream-filled chocolate and his glass of Monbazillac and the pleasure of unbuttoning the dozen small silk buttons that ran down the back of my Thai silk dress. He came on time. He smiled. He did not mention the programme: no doubt he hoped I had not seen it. He was disingenuous. This, more than the sight of the marital double bed, made me angry. I took care not to show it. I murmured and smiled and charmed as usual. Only when he had undone the last button did I slip away from him.

'"You lied to me," I said. "You and Janice share a double bed."

'Now remember that Timothy Tovey was trained as a diplomat. "We sleep in a double bed," he said. "But do we share it? I am not so sure. And since we are also unsure about the very nature of truth I think it unreasonable of you to believe you can define a lie, and therefore define me as a liar."

'I flung what was left of my wine at him, and the glass hurtled through the air and caught and cracked one of my collection of erotic glass paintings. This one was delicately tender, of lesbians and butterflies sporting in the grass; Lesbos innocent and fragile as it was seen to be in the reign of the young Victoria, from which era the painting originated.

'"Now see what you've done," I wept, and he laughed and held me, and promised to buy me another painting, as if I were a child to be teased, tempted and cajoled. But I was not my father's child for nothing. I knew that just as a new kitten cannot replace a familiar old tomcat, inasmuch as mere charm and prettiness, instant purrings and rubbings, fall short in the balance against the weight and resonance of a tough shared experience, so a new work of art can never replace one carelessly destroyed. I also knew in my heart that the glass painting hardly counted as art, merely as the curious and decorative; but I would not let Timothy know I knew. A tragedy had occurred. There was to be no consolation.

'"It is a bad omen," I wept. "The glass is shattered: your lies shattered it. Now you and I will have seven years' bad luck."

'"Gabriella," he pleaded, "be reasonable. You lost your

temper and threw a glass at the painting, so it cracked. That's all."

'"You are very clear when it comes to describing my actions," I said, "but very obscure when it comes to your own. Well, you are a diplomat. I suppose it is only to be expected. Go home to your wife and practise your diplomatic skills on her. Lie as much as you like to her, but I'll have none of it, or you, for seven years."

'"Darling," he said, "seven years is for mirrors. This is only a piece of painted glass." But he was quite pale. He knew what was coming.

'"Five years, then," I said.

'"Two," he pleaded, and I settled for three.

'I am a woman of my word. I did not see Timothy Tovey again for three whole years. I would not. I unplugged the telephone and shut my ears against the ringing of the doorbell. Presently I went to Corfu, and lived with Stavros until the three years were up. Timothy Tovey always referred to Stavros as "your Greek waiter" in the same tone of voice in which I would refer to Janice as "your poor wife". In fact Stavros owned shipping lines and vineyards. Timothy was right in one sense: he was no gentleman — but that's another story, as a result of which few rules can be formulated, except that the best way of washing linen sheets is in running mountain water. Even though water gushed plentiful and hot-and-cold from gold taps in all of Stavros's many establish-ments, I always had the maids go up the hillsides and do the washing in the traditional way, and the drying likewise. Our bed was scented with thyme and honey. Stavros loved it. Alas, I did not love Stavros. And living with a man who loves

you when you do not love him is ageing.
boredom is the most ageing. But enough on t
Stavros. Hairs grew out of his ears, strong and c

'Now of course I had always known perfectly w
Timothy and Janice would make love from time to time.
could they not? How could the erotic energy generated
Timothy and myself, on top of or beneath the gold-on-black-
on-white lace counterpane, not spill over into other beds? I
would have been insulted had it not. In a feebly-sexed
marriage the cuckolded husband is jealous of the lover, the
deceived wife made unhappy by the mistress, because, poor
wedded things, they receive only what is left over. If the
marriage is strongly sexed lovers and mistresses must grind
their teeth with envy, knowing they exist only to sop up the
overflow. That is a further truth. Another is that monogamy,
amongst interesting and lively people, is rare. Or, conversely,
that only those who lack energy, or courage, are faithful. No, I
took offence because it suited me to do so, because the routine
of our life had become too steady for the preservation and
maintenance of romantic love, and, quite instinctively, I knew
the time had come to upset it. In my absence, deprived of
cream-filled chocolates, Timothy Tovey became quite slim.
Janice's diet plan for her husband suddenly began to work. I
daresay she wondered why.'

At this point Miss Sumpter's voice failed again. I beg
readers to remember that she saw life from the balcony of a St
John's Wood villa, and that in spite of what the pinner priests
may say, to be dead is not necessarily to be wise. The voice
from the grave may mislead. My own wife is a very fine, brave
and interesting woman, and I am convinced the very model of
sexual propriety. She is a botanist, and would be ashamed to

live as Gabriella Sumpter lived. Miss Sumpter, it seems, never had anything so vulgar or demanding as a *job* in her entire life.

When Miss Sumpter's voice resumed she was giving instructions as to the removal of scorch stains from white linen. 'Take $\frac{1}{2}$ pint of vinegar', she said, '2 oz. Fuller's earth, 1 oz. of dried fowl dung, $\frac{1}{2}$ oz. of soap and the juice of two large onions. Boil all together to the consistency of paste: spread the composition thickly over the damaged part, and if the threads are not too far gone, or actually consumed by fire, every trace of scorching will disappear after the article has been washed once or twice'. Miss Sumpter says she had Frieda Martock use this method on the tablecloths from the linen cupboard which were badly scorched by the fire at Covert House, and very successful it had been. The fire she referred to was, presumably, the one started by her would-be seducer, Walter James, in which her father, Sir William Lacey-Sumpter, died. The greater part of Covert House, the family home, had not only been totally destroyed but was totally uninsured. One staircase remained, untouched by the flames, and the linen cupboards tucked under it survived, by one of those quirks of happenstance which so often attend disasters. The recipe for the removal of scorch marks came from Miss Sumpter's grandmother's work-book, which happened to be at the Town Museum, for restoration, at the time of the fire. The pinner priests say that one of the phenomena of this kind of replay is what they call the 'trauma splurge effect' – the sub-plot, as it were, spilling back during replay into the major scenarios of life. But I am not sure that what we have here is a case of trauma splurge. I suspect Miss Sumpter of regarding the loss of a tablecloth and the loss of a father as fairly equal tragedies. Thank the GSWITS that my wife, Honor, pays little attention to what she puts over her head in the morning in the way of clothes, or the way the curtains hang; just so long as everything is neat and clean, that's enough for her.

'Walter James,' Miss Sumpter goes on, presently, 'said he wanted to marry me, and I, being only sixteen and knowing little about either life or love, believed him. He was a dark young man with glowing eyes and a haunted expression – the Byronic type, in fact, which experience was to teach me to dislike and distrust. But a young girl all too easily mistakes neurosis for sensitivity, stupidity for courage, duplicity for subtlety and simple insanity for ardour. "He is after the house as much as you," my father warned me. "He is after your inheritance; after the Rembrandts and the Renoirs: their value will increase with age, as yours will diminish. He is a young man who thinks a lot about money." But quite how much neither of us realised!

'I disliked my father for saying this, naturally, and paid little attention to him, because I loved the way that Walter James pressed his full lips on my soft mouth, and delicately inserted his tongue between my virgin teeth, as a promise of so much, so much more to come, if only I would. . . . His male hand upon my female breast! I had always known, from the moment of their first springing, that this, and not the messy, animal drippings of lactation, was their point and purpose. Breasts spoil the hang of a dress quite dreadfully: there must, I had always supposed, be some great recompense in store to make up for it, and now, with Walter James's long, brown fingers laid across their rising whiteness, I knew what it was. My father's voice no longer sounded clear and firm but blurred and indistinct, the mere monkey-chattering of a distant generation.

'I had no mother to advise me as to whether Walter James was or was not sincere in his protestations of love. I must tell you about my mother's death. I was eight. Emerald and I were together on the lawns of Covert House. It was late summer: the sun cast long shadows. I was sitting on a practical twill-covered cushion, wearing a finely woven cotton dress smocked over the bodice with yellow thread and with a yellow sash, drinking squeezed orange juice from a fluted glass. (To remove fruit spots, first cold-soap the article, then touch the spot with a paintbrush dipped in chlorite of soda, and dip instantly into cold water, to prevent injury to the fabric.) My mother was sitting in a pretty white-painted Coalbrookdale wrought iron chair. She sipped champagne. She wore a green dress, and her pretty arms were bare and very white. Her face was shaded, against even the late sun, with a straw hat. She knew how bad a strong light is for the complexion. It is always unwise to drink champagne out-of-doors — wasps love it so — and perhaps it was because of the brim of the hat that she did not see the insect struggling in the liquid, and sipped. The wasp stung her throat, and she was dead, poor, pretty, inconsequential thing, within minutes.

'Seeing her struggle for life, I went running indoors to fetch my father, who I knew was in the house, and found him in his dressing room, naked, on the bed, half hidden by the red velvet cover, half not, with someone I thought for one terrible moment was Nanny McGorrah, but proved to be only Sue Sansippy, my rather elegant governess. My father disengaged himself at once and pulled on his clothes in a great hurry, but by the time he reached my mother she was dead. Sue Sansippy left our employ soon afterwards: my father required her to go. In his mind, I think, he held her responsible for my mother's

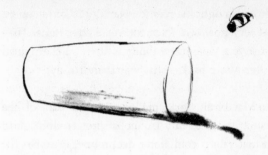

death — though how, reasonably, could either he or she be to blame for the wasp sting? Except, I suppose, had my mother been beneath my father and not Sue Sansippy, she would not have been sipping champagne out-of-doors, in the late summer sun when the wasps are sleepy.

'I spilt my orange drink in my agitation: Nanny McGorrah later tried to remove the stains with calcium hypo-chlorite but left the paste on too long and the fabric went into holes. I was very annoyed, for it was my favourite dress, and told my father it was time the woman went back to the peat-bogs where she belonged — she was ignorant and a barbarian. My father dismissed her at my insistence. I think he gave her a good reference: I hope so. She was messy and incompetent, but had a good heart. I cried over Nanny McGorrah's departure, although I had caused it, as I failed to cry at my mother's funeral. Some tears were owed the God, it seemed:

he claimed them one way or another. And I daresay that I, as my father did when he sent away Sue Sansippy, was sacrificing what I loved best, to abate somehow the pain of my mother's death; to right the balance. Nanny McGorrah wrote me letters every now and then, for years afterwards. They were full of love and concern, thinly written on cheap lined paper. I never wrote back. What was there to say?

'Nanny McGorrah, incidentally, was not part of the joyous throng, the heavenly troupe of friends who joined with me in my transit from life to death. I imagine she is at some lower, less blissful level of existence — for I can imagine nothing more blissful than this! Perhaps she is blotted out altogether? Yet Nanny McGorrah was a good woman: it was not her fault that her belly hung over her white drawers. It seems it is not the wicked who are punished, merely the dull and the ugly. That is another of the rules.'

Sometimes I think Miss Sumpter says these things simply to annoy me; or, more rationally, that the pinner priests misrecorded her on purpose. They are famous for their cynicism. They refuse to acknowledge or admire that human aspiration to incorporate and control the baser instincts which separates us from the beasts. I try but I cannot in the end believe it is merely *luck* that dooms us to be this member or that of the Universal Cast. Free-will must play some part: must refine our lines, our actions and our reactions. The GNFR, we are told, is the religion of acceptance and self-understanding: its credo is that we must strive to comprehend the sub-text of our lives while delivering the text with gusto and without doubt, and that is all very well. But to accept Miss Sumpter's claim that the likes of Nanny McGorrah simply wink out; that, as the script of eternal life pours from the cosmic Word Processor, some vindictive search-and-recall mechanism dictates that her name simply vanishes from all ensuing copies — no, I won't have it.

Or it may be my fault? The rewind is already degenerating, and my fingers may not play over the console with sufficient dexterity to obtain accurate results. Perhaps in some way my own personality plays into the text? I may be a more cynical person than I suppose. Nothing, they say, can ever truly be known. An atom perceived is very different from an atom unperceived!

Miss Sumpter, fortunately, now forgets about the vexed question of Nanny McGorrah's survival in the next life and goes on to relate the events which led up to the fire.

'My father,' she says, 'was right in suspecting Walter James's motives, but wrong in attributing them to greed. What he wanted, in the end, was not money, not me, but revenge upon my father. There was of course no inheritance in existence; my father deluded himself in thinking there was. This was how it happened. Papa had employed young Mr James, a philosophy student from Edinburgh University, to re-arrange his library. There was no money to pay his wages, but Papa did not see fit to mention this at the interview. The world had moved on, since the war, in a way my father could neither countenance nor accept. Tailors now required gentlemen to settle their bills, tradesmen would have the temerity to come knocking at the front door for their money; banks would require stock and even land to be sold to pay off overdrafts. Covert Hall, which once stood proudly at the centre of two hundred and fifty acres, now stood out of all proportion in the merest garden. The house was mortgaged, the horses were gone: as were the Renoirs and Rembrandts Papa spoke of – though naturally he regarded their absence as temporary.

'Papa, you see, was a gambler: a poker player of style and distinction. He assumed that what he had lost he would presently win back: that the mortgaging of the house was the mere turning of a card in a Monopoly game. No doubt, on that late summer evening I have spoken of, he gambled on the time it would take my mother to drink her champagne and come looking for him, and the time it would take him to satisfy his own and Sue Sansippy's sexual needs, and thought the latter would be quicker. He reckoned without the wasp, just as he would reckon without the Queen of Diamonds or the Ace of Spades, which would keep appearing by some unreasonable decree of fate in the hands of his opponents. He was the kind of gambler who took more pleasure in losing grandly than in winning meanly. There is little joy, after all, in simply *winning* twenty thousand pounds – for the money represents neither skill nor labour, nor any kind of real endeavour, so it cannot be experienced as any kind of reward, but there is great emotion and drama in *losing* such a sum before supper, and then going on to lose the last bottle of brandy in the cellar after supper, thus confirming doom and despond. The real gambler, I am convinced, *wants* to lose. My father was a man of great charm and power of persuasion. I stayed on at my boarding school for two extra years because he persuaded my headmistress, Miss Arabella Jeason, to gamble the outstanding fees, and won. More, he would come down to collect me on the Friday (if term ended on the Saturday, which it usually did) and stay overnight, and Miss Jeason would appear flushed and pretty on the platform to wish us all a good and virginal holiday before we dispersed.

'"My darling," Walter James would say to me, from the top of the library ladder, where he perched, sorting the brown books. (Brown books is the trade term for books with antique leather binding: in those post-war years they had little value, and were burnt on bonfires if they were in the way or too dusty. It is only lately that they have been seen to have value.) "Let you and me seal our love as lovers should!"

'Of course I knew what he was talking about — I had seen my father at it often enough. My father never locked doors: he liked to gamble with his privacy, and was, as we knew, an inveterate and triumphant loser. Oh, I was tempted! I had felt the rosy lips of young Walter James on mine, felt his strong hand on my white breast: these matters, once begun, I knew, contained within them the energy of their own conclusion. I loved him; or at any rate the phrase ran round and round in my girlish head like a silver ribbon wrapped around some exquisite gift. This thing called love, for which I had been born! How simple and strong seemed then the word, which now, forty-five years of life and three months of death later, seems so full of complexity and pain.

'"*Please, please!*" begged Walter James, from the top of the library ladder. And I stood gazing up at him, and wondering. I wore a blue and white checked gingham dress, white belted, as befitted my virgin state. Walter James descended. It was evening: the late summer sun streamed in through mullioned windows, and the usually dark and sombre room glowed with warmth and life. There fell upon it that still hush of expectation which always occurs when the God Eros himself draws near.

'"*I don't know, I don't know,*" I wailed.'

Now there are some people, as we know, whose lives proceed by cliché. These are the bit-part actors of the universe whose parts the GSWITS has not had the time or the will to develop. Nevertheless it is remarkable how, when it comes to describing love, Miss Sumpter's language becomes so honeyed and absurd. *Mullioned windows! Dark and sombre room! Hush of expectation! The God Eros draws near!* It's the pinner priests again, no doubt, working overtime in their efforts to make us forget the gritty realities of the present, which are gloomy and urgent indeed. International tensions are worse than ever; though we are used to that. Now it is all talk of radiation, acid rain and the hole above Antarctica through which the ozone layer escapes — and so the priests do their best to draw us into the alternative (and more believable) fictional realities. And yet, and yet! It was on such an evening as Gabriella describes that, thirty years ago, I proposed to my dear Honor. We were visiting Longleat. The late summer sun did indeed shine low through mullioned windows, striking such a beam of light into that dark and sombre room that there was no way we could deny our love, or that God (as we called him then, in those simpler, less argumentative days) had blessed us.

'"Please, Gabriella," said Walter James, "*I shall die if I can't have you. You have no idea how it hurts!*" The year was 1956. Now in those days it was considered very unhealthy for men, physically and mentally, to be sexually aroused and then not satisfied. Men were convinced of it, naturally, and women quite seriously believed it. As for self-satisfaction, that was out of the question since — as some said — it made a man blind, or at the very least — as others said — it rendered a man impotent. So once a girl had, as it were, aroused and excited a man (and she could do that simply by existing, let alone standing staring up at him in a warmly glowing library in a blue and white checked dress, so virginal as to challenge a man's virility) it was her duty to satisfy that need. And yet, once she had done so, it was his equal duty to despise and reject her as being *no good*. Thus, torn between the desire for sex and the desire for love — which in those days were mutually exclusive until that moment the marriage vows were exchanged, when by magic and the grace of God they became one and the same thing — I stood undecided. I wanted Walter James now, this minute. But also I wanted him for ever. How was it to be achieved? Tears ran down my smooth young cheeks from large grey, black-fringed eyes. Walter James put his arms around me.

'"*Don't cry,*" he begged. "*I don't want to make you cry. It's just I love you so much.*"

'I pulled away from him, although the warmth of his embrace was all I wanted.

'"*Give me time,*" I pleaded.

'"*Time!*" he said. "*Every second that passes increases my agony. Don't you understand that?*"

'"*But you'll despise me.*"

'"*Despise you? How could I ever despise you?*" As soon as my father had paid him, he said, we'd run off together. We'd be married.

'"*But I'm only sixteen. My father won't let me.*"

'He said we'd go to Gretna Green. We could marry from there without my father's consent.

'"*But how will we live?*"

'"*On sunshine, and love.*"

'One hand was inside my dress, the other moving up my skirt. I had a sudden memory of Father McCree, and his white podgy hands and his story of the stained girl, and I broke away, confused.

'"*No*," I said. "*No*." But I did not think that would be the end of it.

'Nor was it.

'That evening, as I prepared potato soup in the kitchen — the garden, though for two years unattended by any gardener, still yielded the occasional vegetable — I heard the sound of angry voices up above, in the big drawing room. My father, in a poker game the previous evening, had won back two Renoirs, a Van Dyke and a very large and boring Gainsborough, and was now, with the help of young Walter James, busy re-hanging them in the less faded squares in faded wallpaper which marked their proper place. My father was elated; he felt, no doubt, that his luck had changed. He had no notion, I daresay, that in fact his luck, like his time, was running out.

'As the two men carried in the Gainsborough, a gloomy scene of hills, trees, running water and dwarfed and toiling peasants, Walter James asked my father whether he could not see his way to paying him the three weeks' money he was owed.

'My father raised his eyebrows at the vulgarity of such a request, and did not reply. This clearly angered Walter, who set down one end of the Gainsborough with a jolt which my father could not forgive. My father was the kind of man who, standing on a bridge in flooded Florence, and faced with the alternative of plucking from the swirling waters a drowning child or a sinking Greek statue, would instinctively choose the

latter. But Walter was the kind of man who did not like having money owed to him. That night the three of us dined together, on thick potato soup, sprinkled with parsley, and a good claret — the kind my father referred to as 'decent', with that one-upmanship of wine snobs which leaves superlatives only to the ignorant. He had won a case of claret the previous week. He was, or so he thought, onto a winning streak.'

Miss Sumpter's voice faded and reformed into what I can only describe as her laundry-litany. This short period of her life, when her father's gambling had reduced the family fortunes to such an extent that she was obliged to be not merely skivvy and cook but laundrymaid too, seems to have coloured her life so that the dye runs, as it were, back and forwards in time, and stains all her recollections, as a single red garment, put into a white wash, will render everything forever pink. (I use this metaphor with some feeling, as my dear Honor recently put my new red football shorts in the washing machine with my white underclothing and turned the dial to 'hot wash', with obvious results!)

Both men, Miss Sumpter observed, were wearing not so much white as whitish shirts during the course of their quarrel. She learned a lesson, she claims, that she has never forgotten. White must always be washed with white if it is to remain white, and not turn instead to one of that range of colours one sees at dawn on a pebbly sea-washed beach — greys and buffs and duns and pinky-yellow and purply-blue and yellowy-pink, and the peculiar grey-to-blue that characterises a drizzly sea dawn. Let there not be a single stripe, a single spot, a single stray grey sock or tartan-bordered handkerchief, implores Miss Sumpter, that goes with the white wash into the tub or into the machine, or pure whiteness will be lost forever. Heavily soiled cotton and linen whites must of course be pre-washed before being allowed into contact with more delicate fabrics – woollens and silks and polyesters and so forth: even so, and although quite a quantity of the heavier, tougher fabrics may be allowed to press up close in the wash with one another, be tumbled this way and that and still not lose their purity, it is preferable to wash a white blouse, or white stockings, or a white shirt, quite separately. Let a flimsy handful of fabric have a whole tub or machine to itself: let it seethe and swirl and rinse free: and peg it outside in cool blowing air to dry. (But never, remember, if there is a scrap of nylon in it, never *ever* hang out white clothing in direct sunlight, for it will yellow at once!) And it may seem profligate of time and soap powder, electricity and machine wear-and-tear to launder this way – if every white blouse, every cream shirt is to have a whole wash to itself – but it must be done! If Gabriella Sumpter found one of the servants saving time and money by not sorting the laundry properly, the said sloven would, she tells us, be dismissed at once.

Miss Sumpter did not mention whether or not the many dismissed servants who have littered her life turned up in the joyous throng who escorted her from this life to the next. No.

Miss Sumpter lets us know, first, then, that both men, her father and her suitor, were wearing badly washed shirts at dinner on that fatal night. She speaks rather as if this should be read as an omen of bad luck. Not to look after objects, artefacts or clothing properly seems inevitably, in Miss Sumpter's account of her life, to lead to chaos and distress. It is a faulty view of the world: it is a preoccupation with trivia which can only appear luxurious, in the old sense of that word. The times are out of sympathy with those who live off the fat of the land and never do a hand's turn in their lives. I am more than ever opposed to the GNFR's determination to go public with the Sumpter re-wind. What do we want? A whole nation of washerwomen, firm in their belief that cleanliness is not only next to Godliness but will lead to immortality? There is no shortage of re-winds from which to choose — up and down the country the graveyards are noisy and tumultuous with spirits demanding to be heard. Honor said in bed only last night that in her opinion the Day of Judgement had been and gone, unnoticed by the living: that the Christian era had now passed formally and not just informally away. The GNFR has become the established religion of the land, rather to its own surprise; now it must conduct itself with due regard to its responsibilities. But back to Miss Sumpter!

Over dinner, it seems, her father taunted the young philosopher, accused him not just of literal virginity, but worse, of financial innocence as well, and dared him to gamble the three weeks' missing wages against Covert Hall plus contents. The young man accepted the bet. He wagered on the number of potatoes used by Gabriella to make the soup. Gabriella was to write the number on a folded piece of paper. This she did. She wrote the number twelve, although in fact she had used merely eight potatoes — four large wormy ones and four that were small, withered and sprouting — and then cheated, making more of the soup by thickening with a flour and water paste. This, of course, she could not admit to. She hated peeling potatoes, especially when they were not in the best of condition. And in this I don't blame her. Even Honor never peels potatoes if she can help it.

'Eight,' said her father.

'Twelve,' said Walter James.

And in this manner Walter James won his wager.

Sir William bit his lip.

'How many peas in a Birds Eye Jumbo packet?' he demanded, harshly.

'The matter is irrelevant,' said Walter James, loftily, 'since you have nothing left to wager.'

'A man has always something left to wager; you are young in the ways of gambling if you believe otherwise.'

'But nothing that I want, now I have everything.'

Sir William smiled.

'My daughter,' said Sir Lacey-Sumpter. 'What about my daughter? My daughter against the return of Covert Hall. Have everything, young man, or nothing.'

'Gabriella?' Walter James was quite pale. 'Gamble Gabriella?'

'Gabriella,' said his lordship, firmly.

'You're on,' said Walter.

Gabriella stopped weeping. She counted out the peas. There were 748. She wrote the number down, accurately this time.

'730,' said Walter.

'768,' said Sir William. And so Walter, being the nearest by two peas, won Gabriella as well as Covert Hall. Gabriella was overwhelmed by joy. Not only was she relieved of the responsibility of her own life but might have Walter James as well, guiltlessly.

But now his lordship took off his shirt.

'No,' said Walter, 'this is where we stop. I do not *want* your shirt.'

'My shirt against Covert Hall. You have Gabriella, but I have nowhere to live. I might, for once, have gone too far! As for you, Mr James, you need a clean shirt more than anything!' (Though, indeed, his was in no better state than Walter's. But when does a man look closely at the stains on his own shirt?)

'I daresay I have nothing to lose,' said Walter, 'tonight luck is with me!' and over the comparative speed of two raindrops coursing down the windowpane he there and then lost Covert Hall. The upkeep of the place, for any responsible person, would have been formidable, and perhaps Walter James knew it.

Thus Gabriella Sumpter became the victim of her father's mania for gambling.

'How could you, father!' she wept, as the young man led her away. She felt some protest was necessary.

'My dear,' her father said, 'be reasonable. The young man is certainly owed something. He has done an excellent job on the library. Your dear mother, God rest her soul, would agree that it is a daughter's duty to honour her father's debts.' Somewhat embarrassed, Sir Lacey-Sumpter took to inspecting the Gainsborough for possible damage, humming and hah-ing the while — a flake of paint missing here, a minute scratch there? His daughter virgin no more, but a woman of the world — a consummation devoutly to be wished! Some men, observes Miss Sumpter, see virginity in women, even in their own daughters, as an affront to the whole male sex.

I should, I suppose, let Miss Sumpter now take up her own account, but I feel obliged to clip and censor just a little. I will let her resume presently — not yet. I am no prude, but this piece of incest-by-proxy can only increase the sum of prurience presently adrift in the world. Too much permissiveness spoils the story! There is, we must always remember, a two-way process between the creator and the created — the latter can, by effort and example, teach the GSWITS a thing or two, cure the perpetual drift towards explicitness. Pornography is a cheap and nasty way of making a quick effect: we know Our Writer is capable of better things: or always try to believe this is the case.

What happened was that Walter James, having made Gabriella Sumpter feel as guilty as he could and after removing her clothes, attempted to take her virginity. Only he was unable so to do. His manhood, faced with the reality of the young woman, quite deserted him. Enraged because, having thrown away the house, he could not properly possess the daughter of the house, he strode into Sir Lacey-Sumpter's bedroom in the middle of the night and demanded that they renegotiate their wager.

'Never!' cried Sir Lacey-Sumpter, sitting up naked in the chilly room. He seldom wore night-clothes, which gave Gabriella an unwelcome and extra task when it came to washing the sheets. As Honor keeps reminding our children, pyjamas are there to save the sheets, quilt covers to save the quilts. Use them!

'At least give me my three weeks' wages!' the young man demanded, beside himself with rage, but the older man refused even that. He merely abandoned all hope of sleep, pulled on his shirt and went downstairs, followed by the furious Walter and the pleading Gabriella, opened another bottle of claret, poured himself a glass, and drank without offering the young man so much as a drop. But his hand trembled in his displeasure so that he spilled wine down his chin and staining drops fell upon his already discoloured shirt, and onto the white chest hairs which buttons broken by too harsh a wash revealed.

'You had your chance and blew it,' Sir Lacey-Sumpter said to the young man, who promptly left the house, threatening revenge. Gabriella, doubly betrayed, insulted, humiliated and found wanting (or so she felt) by the man she loved (or thought she loved), was sent sobbing off to bed.

'I shouldn't have done it,' she admits on the tapes. 'I should have stayed and seen to both men's shirts. White wine spotted over red, then well washed, will often do the trick!'

She weeps here. The tape shivers. The voice falters. We are at the moment of trauma.

She was roused in the night by the crackle of burning timbers and the acrid smell of smoke — Walter James had set fire to the house, or such is the assumption that must be made, although his act of arson was never proved. Gabriella, wrapped in a sheet and with white furry mules upon her little feet, escaped into the grounds. Her father, going back into the house to rescue the Gainsborough, was crushed beneath a falling beam even as he dragged the picture to safety — the frame survived, although the painting itself was scorched beyond repair. The insurance on the house had, of course, run out and not been renewed. Gabriella was left, within the space of an hour, orphaned, homeless and penniless: she owned nothing but the sheet in which she was wrapped and the little white fluffy mules upon her feet — and these were now badly grass-stained, for the water from the firemen's hoses and the trampling of male feet had churned up the once smooth lawn on which she stood.

Gabriella was taken in by a certain Dr Aldred Ray, the quiet, brilliant assistant to the local physician, who comforted her, fed her, nurtured her, clothed her, unclothed her, took her into his narrow bachelor bed and found her not in the least wanting. Miss Sumpter goes quite thoroughly into the detail of this new seduction, but I shall refrain from so doing, for reasons already given.

'As one house is razed to the ground,' suffice it for Miss Sumpter to say, 'another one opens its doors. Life casts you down then lifts you up. One lover departs, another waits on the doorstep. I thought at the time,' she adds, 'that I would never find a lover better than Dr Aldred Ray; that such a one could hardly exist. But of course I was wrong! One of the great rewards of my life has been the discovery that there is always a better lover than the last.'

Oh Miss Sumpter, shame! And here indeed the tape crackles again. Again the tears, then a pause and a gasp. Miss Sumpter weeps, steadies, speaks again. But she is not, when it comes to it, lamenting the frivolity of her life.

'Why I weep now', says Miss Sumpter, 'is simply because I did not weep at the time. I was too happy with Dr Ray to pay proper attention to my father's death, either to grieve or to consider the great insult he had done me by gambling me away, or the manner in which he had, all but directly, been responsible for my mother's death. I, who in life recalled little, who when asked about my childhood described it unthinkingly as a time of bliss, remember all too much in death. Perhaps this post mortem paradise is not so nicely sharp-edged and contained as I had thought, but dim around the edges, as memories crowd in. They make a veritable fog: I must find my way through, I must make sense of my life. I grope, I ache, I yearn! It is painful, all so painful,' weeps Miss Sumpter.

And as the voice wails on in the agony of recollection, at feelings long unfelt now felt at last, I wish more than ever that the pinner priests had not disturbed this poor, troubled woman, but had simply let her be. Our self esteem is so hardly won! Must we understand and acknowledge everything; must the very ground beneath our feet be forever churned up and trampled? But just when I am raising up my own voice in grief, sorrow and protest, Miss Sumpter's voice resumes again, quite calm, bright and light, cured, untouched by self-knowledge.

'To remove grass stains from fur,' Miss Sumpter is saying, 'proceed in the same way as for removing scorch stains from linen sheets. With a mixture of vinegar, water and fowl dung.'

I feel in myself the dawn of an emotion: soon, if I am not careful, it will dazzle and blind, it will become the brightest, hottest day imaginable: the name of the day would be love. I will have to explain to Honor: I'm sure she won't mind. This tiny little seed — which I will take good care *not* to water — can be no threat to my secure and happy earthly union with her dear good self. In love with a re-wind, a voice from the grave? Absurd! Honor will tell me it's absurd, and the uneasiness will be swept away in a gale of commonsense. Am I mixing my metaphors? I fear I am. See, I am already under Miss Sumpter's influence! Too late!

And think again! Does the GNFR not tell us that no seed should be left unwatered, no cake uncooked, no telephone call unanswered? Does it not insist that all experience must be savoured, all emotion fully acknowledged? That it is only the outcome of sexual attraction, that is to say its fulfilment, which is to be cautiously approached, lest it lead to the premature end of the story and not its lengthy continuation. Do they not hold that an unspoken, secret love is the best love of all? Gratifying to him or her who nurtures it, causing no trouble to anyone around? Indeed the GNFR does! So I shall allow myself to love secretly. Yes. I shan't tell Honor; I shall simply let love gnaw away like a worm in the bud. It's quite safe. Time stands between Gabriella Sumpter and myself – the steady tick, tick, tick of the falling decades intervenes. Gabriella lives, weeps, feels, and yet is dead and buried. I cannot touch her, cannot have more than an inner corporeal reaching, body to soul, soul to body; her voice lives in my head, not hers. Gabriella, my love.

There, it's said! GSWITS, have mercy upon us, even as we have mercy upon you! So goes our prayer. Forgive us as we forgive you. Learn from us as we learn from you. Accept me as I strive to accept you, forgiving you for the fault of making me ill-favoured, humourless and self-righteous. Gabriella, my love!

'Well,' says Miss Sumpter, 'what happened just then? I seemed almost to pass out: I heard again the strange silence that descends when mere physical attraction passes into love: the blotting out of the physical world, the approach of the real one. Aldred told me this was probably the effect of phenylalanine, the hormone which is secreted in extra quantity in the brains of those who fall in love – that same hormone which disturbs appetite, makes the eye shine, the skin glow, the whole body receptive to sexual activity, and is as addictive as heroin. (It is a substance found in chocolate, incidentally, which is why, they say, chocolates are the favourite gifts of suitors. *Only taste this, and you will love me!*) It is quite possible, said Aldred, that with the first surge of phenylalanine the hearing areas of the brain are affected, and that this, and nothing more, is what the nuministic sense of quiet, as of the God descending, is all about. He may be right. It does not worry me one way or another. I do not think the effect is one whit diminished because the cause can be understood. And I have no brain any more, no body, and still I hear it. It outlasts even death.

'How happy Aldred and I were in our country cottage. I look back upon those days with pleasure. Roses grew around the door, and there was money enough for proper household help. Our house was small, and seemed smaller to me because I was accustomed to moving about in the grand if neglected rooms of Covert Hall. After my mother died, the place had been let go to rack and ruin. The staff never stayed — my father was always reluctant to pay them wages. Either they were, he said, too ugly to deserve any, or, if they were not, then he had slept with them and so felt they should clean up for nothing, as wives do. So, of course, one by one, they left. And I was taken out of school — the headmistress had married and I daresay did not want me about as a constant reminder of her past weakness. Besides, the issue of the owing school fees became, in the end, as money matters do, impossible to fudge — and my father's assumption was that if his wife was dead, and the servants gone — why, then his daughter would see that his meals were on the table, and that there were always clean clothes to put on. A hungry man in a gravy-stained suit may be a fine poker player, but where will he find proper opponents to play against, or any with money worth losing?

'But these matters were now in the past. I resolved to forget my father and my mother, who had both died so dramatically. There is a very pleasant man here, by the way, who died recently in Bengal: a gentle bird-watcher, who took great care, as I did, in life, never to tread on a worm, never to crush an ant or squash a fly. The poor soul was literally eaten by a tiger while pursuing a rare owl into the jungle. Ah, one may admire creation, but one should never trust it. Never believe that it's kind, or it will eat you alive!

'So: Aldred and I lived hand in hand in our cosy cottage, and we had a fine brass bed which took up almost the entire front bedroom. My dear Aldred went out to Dr Lovell's surgery every morning to cure the blind, the halt, the lame and so forth, and I would curl my hair, read books, write verse, press flowers and the like, waiting for his return. It was at this time of my life that Frieda Martock, who lived locally, first started sewing for me: she made a particularly pretty nightdress, I remember, from a cream-coloured muslin, caught under the bosom with a lilac ribbon. At sixteen I had altogether too plump a chest for any hope of elegance, but Aldred was happy enough – more than happy – with me as I was, and Frieda Martock's dressmaking skills were good, so that if I caught sight of myself sideways on I was not necessarily reduced to tears. I wore the nightdress, of course, mostly for the pleasure of having Aldred take it off.

'Coloured muslin requires very delicate treatment, and the nightdress finally came to grief some fourteen years later (having stood up to Aldred well enough, and one or two others besides) at the brutal hands of one of Julia Tovey's maids, who soaked the poor thing overnight along with the heavy wash and (what is more) gaily splashed soda into the

tub, so that by morning the garment was scarcely cream at all but a dreary greyish-white. It should of course have been washed separately, and quickly, then rinsed in softened water, in which common salt had been dissolved — in the mild proportion of a handful to three or four gallons — and wrung gently as soon as rinsed, with as little twisting as possible, before being immediately hung out to dry.

'When the Tovey maid had the face to hand me back, ironed and folded and flattened, the poor, ruined, de-natured garment, I did not bother to reproach her. I simply went straight to Julia and said:

'"Lady Tovey, I am at a loss to understand why you worry so much about your son's association with me. Nothing as lamentable as this would ever happen in a household over which *I* had control."

'I left her dribbling and boggling — she had a heavy jaw, which always seemed to me oddly loose — and made Timothy choose between me and her. He chose me, as I knew he would. I had hoped not to have forced the issue — there is nothing so dreary or repetitive as the conversation of a man torn by guilt — but I took the destruction of my nightdress (wilful or otherwise) as an omen. That is another of the rules. *Little things are sent to warn us.* A car which won't start, or a log fire which sends smoke back into the room, milk souring in a jug, scrambled eggs burned — any trivial event which comes between the pleasure of two lovers foreshadows the wider breach. Nothing is without meaning. We whirl through our galaxy, matter and spirit hopelessly confused; a ball shot through with lightning streaks of good and bad, strands forever flying out from the central mass, then drifting back in towards it, trapped by the sheer gravity of animation; by the very energy of this great tumbling globe of being.'

I longed to ask Miss Sumpter more about the nature of the 'central mass', but if the pinner priests have solved the secret of direct communication with the departed they are keeping it to themselves. I could listen but I could not, as I suspect they can, enquire. It is, I grant, important and sensible for the priests of any religion to maintain a body of arcane knowledge, and when the Revised Great New Fictional Religion takes over I daresay we will have our secrets too; that is only prudent. As it happened, Miss Sumpter seemed to sense my enquiry. When she spoke next I had the clear sensation that she was addressing her remarks directly to me.

'I can only compare the central globe to that pile of tangled threads to be found at the bottom of a neglected sewing box, but seized up, multiplied by infinity and sent spinning through the cosmos by an immense force. Amongst these tangles we spend our lives. Our task is the disentangling of the threads. They should never have got into this state in the first place.'

Oh, my beloved Miss Sumpter: your delicate fingers, plucking and pulling at my heart! If only you and I had been written into the same script; if only we had shared the same decades. I know you can feel my spirit, pressing in on yours, as I feel yours upon mine: we have been divided by time, by the error of the GSWITS or, more likely, of the Divine Typist who sitteth at His right side. Error, simple error, which by a malign fate dogs the footsteps of the GSWITS, and so dogs the course of all our lives! I would have made you happy, Gabriella – you would have borne my children . . . No! Stop – it must stop. Since my sessions here in the British Museum with the Sumpter Tapes I have been brusque and unkind to dear Honor. Not her fault she is so solid and practical, compared to the divine translucence of Gabriella Sumpter, re-wound, re-called, re-played. I must not forget that Honor is the mother of my children, and mothers perforce must end up as sensible people. They have no choice. How can I wish children upon Gabriella? Instead, I send curses on the Tovey maidservant, who dared to spoil my Gabriella's muslin nightdress.

What happened to Gabriella and her beloved Dr Aldred was this. They could not marry, since he had contracted an unfortunate marriage at the age of eighteen and the laws of the land did not at that time allow for divorce by the desire of only one of the partners. Nevertheless, he bought her a wedding ring and she wore it proudly, and the village, in its kindness and goodwill, forbore to ask the young couple too many questions. As well as his medical work, Aldred was doing research into the epidemiology of infantile meningitis, a disease which plagued the neighbourhood: he would work late, late into the night, poring over pages of statistics, and Gabriella would sit by him as he worked, stroking his cheek, biting his ear – and he would of course break off from time to time to embrace her. (The sexual act, Miss Sumpter observed, is a great stimulant to the intellect.) As a result of their joint labours the local epidemic was stopped, a national epidemic prevented, and the young doctor became famous – though not of course rich.

'Another of the rules', Gabriella observes, 'is that virtue *is* its own reward. *No one becomes rich by doing good.* Aldred gave up his country practise and he and I moved to London where he could the better continue his research. Aldred's mother bought us a mean little flat in Hackney, within walking distance of the Mile End Research Institute. The beds were damp. Aldred's mother was both a Catholic and a militant socialist, and did not, frankly, like me: no doubt she thought Aldred should have stayed with his boring wife and children and been a humble country doctor for ever. But people must, of course, aspire: there is no stopping them, no preventing them, if that is in their nature. Aldred's mother should have saved her breath to cool her porridge. He was her only child. She wished to make him in her own image: a Christ amongst the sufferers. She could see in me, I expect — apart from the sheer youth and erotic energy which had, or so she thought, seduced her son away from the stony path she had laid out for him — that nature, so contrary to her own, which despises sufferers, which believes the halt, the lame and the old are better put out of their misery quickly, leaving the world to those who best inherit it. No wonder the beds she provided were damp!

'According to my grandmother's book there are few things more dangerous than damp beds. No bed should ever be allowed to become so. The moist air of a damp bed carries away the natural heat of a body with the most dangerous rapidity. The body becomes chilled; disease, and often death, ensue. *Sit up all night rather than sleep in a damp bed*, my grandmother advised. *Or, if you are only suspicious of dampness and wish for a night's rest, wrap yourself in a blanket and cover yourself with all the clothes you can find, so as to allow no escape of heat.* After I had spent several nights so covered up, Aldred agreed that we should move to a house more suitable to my tastes, with rooms of a decent size, and a staff flat, so the servants could keep themselves to themselves, and not intrude on our bliss. I found just such a house in Orme Square, tucked in behind Hyde Park and Queensway. Wisteria hung its purple fronds over low windows; there was a little iron gate: I knew we would be happy there.

'Aldred was worried about the general expense and the distance from his work, so I contrived to find him a post in Harley Street, which was only just around the corner, as assistant to Mr Clive Cunningham, the famous cosmetic surgeon. Everyone, I think, must take shifts at virtue. Aldred had saved the country from the scourge of meningitis: now he deserved to have some comfort, and some fun. The ailments of the rich, I always think, are easier to accept than the illnesses of the poor. And, the rich being more sensitive, the relief of their suffering is just as gratifying to the doctor. What's more, the financial rewards are better! To sit up night after night as young lovers in a country cottage is one thing; to sit up in a damp-bedded Hackney slum quite another. It simply could not be. I would go up to Mr Cunningham's rooms after surgery hours. He was a man of great charm and persuasion – though if my dear Aldred was twice my age he was as old again.

'Such interesting and well-paid employment as Aldred had been fortunate enough to acquire did not then and does not now come easily, and I had made certain promises to Mr Cunningham, and kept them – I must say perhaps with a little more enthusiasm than was strictly necessary. The fact was that as Aldred advanced in his profession, as he became more prosperous, he became duller. The fiery, dedicated young man who rescued me from distress and destitution made a far better and more romantic lover than the young surgeon who charmed matrons into facelifts! And, do remember, I was not married to Aldred; he had put the house in my name, in recompense, but what are the obligations of gratitude compared to the obligations of marriage? Oh, very few! And that, perhaps, is why I never chose to marry.

'I was still fond of Aldred. How sad it is, that we turn those we love into what we want, and then find that what we want we do not love! Easier to love a house, I think, than a person. And what a charming house this was; with its little walled back garden, and its pear tree; and walks across the park to the shops, and riding in Rotten Row, and glasses of wine with theatrical people – I loved the theatre – and, for work, the supervision of the servants, or, for excitement, a visit to Mr Cunningham, perhaps even unannounced.

'His nurse *knew*, of course, and there was always a danger she might tell Aldred. She had to go. Poor woman. It was not, I suppose, her fault; Mr Cunningham claimed she was efficient, and that may be so, but she had a perpetual cold in the nose, and would obviously have been better employed in the public nursing sector, not the private. She reminded me of Nanny McGorrah. To have a head cold, of course, is to weep with the nose instead of with the eyes: it is a mere displacement of grief. The cure is not in aspirin but in self-discovery. Oh, how wearisome life is . . .'

Here her voice breaks again. Poor woman! What is the point of disturbing her? We cannot help what we are: we cannot any of us go back into the past and undo what we have done –

'This place I am in now', says Miss Sumpter, and it seemed to me that at this point her voice began to age alarmingly, 'is a strange kind of paradise indeed. The corridor between life and death is free of guilt, filled only with the marvel of simply being; but here we must try to understand what we are, and why we are: oh, it is all sub-text, it is so difficult ...'

I do suspect the pinner priests of putting words into Miss Sumpter's head. She was not herself a member of the GNFR: concepts such as 'sub-text' must be strange to her. Unless, indeed – and this I find truly exciting – we have it even righter than we know, and the blinding truth of our worldly existence has been revealed to Miss Sumpter after death and through her confirmation and reassurance given back to us. In which case praise be the GSWITS, praise be! Forgive Thou my unbelief!

'Aldred discovered us,' my Gabriella continues, when she had regained her strength. 'I would not have had that happen for the world. I did not want to hurt him. It was just that the danger of being discovered added so greatly to our pleasure: the sound of his calm, wise voice in the next room as Clive's fingers found my nipples, his mouth the parting between my legs, made the action what it was. It dared the God Eros, compelling him to show his presence – but of course one day Aldred opened the door, which Clive had forgotten to lock –

'"I say, Cunningham, old fellow –"'

'And then Aldred saw what he saw. He did not hit his rival but he did hit me. A man seldom hits his superior – whom he sees as having greater status, who earns more than he, and is more attractive than he, having lured his woman away. No, such a man merely bows his head and slinks away, defeated and humiliated. It is the woman he hits, for in their hearts all men despise women, as the cock despises the hen who serves him, as I despise the servants who serve me. Aldred fortunately did not hit me very hard, just enough to perforate an ear-drum and make himself feel guilty. Mr Cunningham departed quickly on an urgent case, leaving Aldred to help me to my feet, to wrap a lace tablecloth – a not very interesting, machine-made piece of lace, and rather grubby – around my naked body.

'"*You are a bully and a ruffian*," I sobbed. "*You will not even marry me; all you do is neglect me! Do you think you have all this*" – and I indicated the sombre splendour of the room – "*for nothing? No, it is thanks to me! And see, you show your gratitude! By hitting me! What sort of love is that? You may apologise, but I will not be able to hear you, because you have made me deaf!*"

'It never does to apologise to men, even when in the wrong. All they remember then is your error. It seals into their minds the fact that you have done something to be sorry for. They will never forget it, and will reproach you to the end of your days. Better far to move the blame from you to them. And when discovered *in flagrante delicto*, the rule is, *never apologise, always justify.*'

Here the voice paused, and this time when it resumed it had become fluttery and desperate: it reminded me of the sound of the wings of a moth trapped near too bright a lamp. 'What are they saying to me? That I am wrong? That the rules of expediency are not the rules of life? What do they mean? Someone, help me! There are blackberry stains – I will never get them out. I have tried chloride of soda, essence of lemon and Dab-it-off and nothing helps. Oh hurry, hurry, before the words fade! Perhaps I have not much time. Perhaps when I am healed I will have nothing to say, or the means to say it?'

But after a short, frightening silence in which I thought the lamp had altogether burned her up, my beloved's voice resumed, young and bright again, as if these frights and warnings had been nothing, were mere passing afflictions. 'I went home and shut the door and would not let Aldred in for a week. How ill, tormented and tired he looked by the time I relented. My ear was quite better by then, or I would not even have considered opening the door. Poor Aldred was beside himself with jealousy and longing. He begged that we should sell the house, and he would forget medicine, and we would go off together – somewhere, anywhere – only we must be together and I must never, never be unfaithful to him again.

'"*Not even for your sake, Aldred? I only did it for you!*"

'"*Not even for my sake. And we will have children: then you will be happy and content –*"

'"*How can we have children? If we can't marry – if she won't divorce you? Don't you see how I have to live, Aldred, disgraced in the eyes of the world? I have to live in the demi-monde. Make my friends amongst artists, writers, actors and other disreputable people, who are all fun and charm, no doubt, but it can hardly count as proper life. They are not proper people. What have you done to me? I came to you an orphaned virgin of sixteen –*"

'He begged me to say no more and actually offered to kill his wife if that would suit me. But I said no, I had no wish to be a murderer's wife. Nor did I have any desire to go to Bolivia, or New Zealand, or any of the other places he suggested. We would stay where we were, and he would go back to work as Mr Cunningham's assistant. Aldred protested that he could never, ever, stand such humiliation as that, but, as I pointed out, he had no choice. Who else would employ him on such favourable terms? Cosmetic surgeons, unlike medical researchers, are interchangeable. I, for my part, vowed never to see Mr Cunningham in private again — nor did I, or only once or twice, when he claimed his hand trembled as he operated from sheer deprivation of me. It does not do to make these emotional breaks too quickly. Another rule: men like to feel that they are doing the giving up. If you are seen to give them up they take offence and can turn quite nasty.

'So now we made it up, dear Aldred and I, and sealed our new beginning with many kisses, and our house grew to feel warm and safe again. I took a degree in Fine Arts at the Courtauld Institute, and Aldred learned, eventually, to work happily with Mr Cunningham, though I think it was a little hard for him. Men are such seekers after status! See two cockerels, fighting over who shall rule the roost, stand crowing in the dung heap, and fluff the feathers of the silly hens! Well might blood flow, for the one who loses hardly lifts his head again to groan, let alone crow, and eats last, on leftovers, and grows thin and wretched, despised even by the lamest, scraggiest hen.

'Aldred is here on the other side: my beloved Aldred is with me. He took my hand as we swept along the corridor between life and death. He took it as a brother would a little sister's: we were warm and safe together. We mistook our roles in life, or they were mistaken for us. How full of error the world is! We should have been family, brother and sister: the sex between us was born simply of youth, energy and proximity. All that we had was great affection, the one for the other — and of course my capacity to cause him pain. Mr Cunningham is over here too. He left cosmetic surgery some time in the early eighties and became a specialist in in-vitro conception and artificial insemination, a venture which ended badly. His clients believed they were being fertilised by the sperm of 'virile young medical students', but in fact of course the sperm was all his, and it was reckoned at the court case that there are some five hundred of his children in Central London alone. Well, why not? And though his clients were disconcerted – indeed, some were appalled – to know that their children had been fathered not by some vaguely imagined Adonis but by this wizened, trembling, short-sighted septuagenarian, they should not have worried. Once indeed and in truth Clive Cunningham had been Adonis enough, and sperm does not acknowledge age. It is forever in its prime.

'Clive Cunningham took my other hand as we swept along the corridor of the dying and I saw a smile pass between him and Aldred in the glow of events that joined us all, in which there was no pain, only connection. I say *smile*, I say *saw*, because these are the only words I have to describe what is beyond words – such feeble, incomplete instruments they are! Let me go, whoever you are! Why do you make me speak, use words where no words belong, only connection? Truly I was mistaken: I have no rules to give you: there is such a tangle in the sewing box! Where does one thread begin, another end? How can I know? Please let me rest in peace!'

My poor Gabriella's voice faded out. She seemed to suffer. I wanted not to hear, but how could I refuse experience? I threw switches and turned dials, almost to overload. I would not let her go.

'Here, see, a strand,' she went on, after a while, as if fingers and mind had been busy un-plaiting. 'A strong one, a central one, around which the tangle forms. Yes – see! – that must be Timothy Tovey. It is plaited and woven and multicoloured; it is shot through with silver and gold. How wonderful it is! But look! Someone has washed him badly, made the water too hot. The colours have run. It need never have happened. Any person can be washed, if proper care and attention is paid, even those which say "Dry Clean Only" – which is mostly only a manufacturer's convenience – oh, my poor head! What is a word, and what is a label, and what is a principle, and who can we trust?...'

Here, for all my efforts, the tape ends, abruptly; and, fortunately, with it the sensuous spell cast over me by that elderly woman, Gabriella Sumpter, dead these three months. Lucky for Honor: how does a woman deal with a husband in love with a re-wind? I have no doubt he moons and picks at his food and longs for death, the sooner to join his beloved, to be part of the joyous throng in the Great Script Conference – for that, I have no doubt, is where Gabriella Sumpter found herself.

Honor would have done her best to keep me in this world, and fed me on dumplings and lemon meringue pie, packet-made. I don't think she has ever washed a garment by hand, let alone ironed one. She does not even possess an iron: she pushes a week's multicoloured laundry into the washing machine and switches it to 'whites, heavy' and gets on with her life. That is why my underclothing is always harsh and pinkish-purplish. But neither would Honor have deceived me with the likes of Clive Cunningham.

I counted my blessings, shook the spell of Gabriella Sumpter from me, and prepared a solid and constructive report on the Sumpter Tapes for the coming GNFR Synod. I argued that they contained no evidence that the GSWITS was attempting to contact his humble creation, or giving us the reassurance we need that we have, indeed, through our

contacts with the re-winds, put our fingers on the meaning of the universe.

The rules of laundry are not the rules of life! I included some fairly strong criticism of the current clique of pinner priests. The report may well be something of a sensation. But I was not finished with Gabriella Sumpter. That night she came to me in a dream: a high-bosomed sixteen-year-old girl in a white dress, singed around the hem, her hair dishevelled, her lovely eyes wild. She begged me to take a message to Janice Tovey, to say there was nothing to grieve about, since everything was part of everything else. How familiar, how sweet her voice was. But I decided I would do nothing; Janice Tovey would hardly welcome such a message. Re-winds are everywhere these days, and the messages they send are not necessarily more sensible in death than in life.

On the following night Gabriella came again, and this time Honor saw her too: the presence in our bedroom was so bright it was as if someone had switched on the light. Honor, usually such a sound sleeper, woke with a start and, seeing a stranger in the room, groped for the teeth she kept in a glass beside the bed. I have no doubt she wanted to look her best, for Gabriella, at some thirty years, was the most ravishing creature I have ever seen, dressed in the cream-coloured muslin nightdress she had spoken of, gathered under perfect breasts with a lilac ribbon, dark hair flowing round the sweetest face.

'Tell Timothy Tovey to hurry,' she said. 'Tell him he is the thread that binds us together.' At that she faded out — but not, I thought, without a slight frown at the grey pinkly-purple state of our bed-linen; though that last may be my imagination.

'Who on earth was that?' Poor Honor was terrified. I explained a little of the story, and she suggested, wisely, that perhaps I should do what I had been asked and get in touch with the Toveys, in case Gabriella next chose to appear in her winding sheet — no matter how beautifully made by Miss Martock — fresh from her grave and deliquesced about the eyes. A horrible thought!

So that is what I did. The Toveys lived in a magnificent house on Hyde Park. It is one of the sadder features of the GNFR that it tends to maintain, indeed even increase, such inequities as already exist between the haves and the have-nots. Although dramatic individual stories of rags to riches, riches to rags, are a common enough feature in Western societies nurtured under the GNFR, on the whole there is little social mobility. The poor just gently get poorer; the rich, not so gently, get richer: our religion seems to breed social passivity. To consent is not to strive. The *idea* is so important in the formation of civilisations, is it not? Notions of socialism and a fair society faded along with Christianity: the eighties finally saw them off. The GSWITS, I fear, is a great admirer of Dickens.

Be that as it may, it was obvious to me that money was the least of the Toveys' worries. Depression, however, may well have been. I saw a Rolls Royce parked in the drive, and a Bentley in the garage, but both in a dull old-fashioned black, not the brilliant spots and swirls so popular these days. The interior of the Toveys' house, though flawlessly decorated, was bleak and reproachful in its grandeur: the very flowers in the vases seemed to sigh and wilt in the unkind light of central chandeliers which sent unflattering shadows through the too-high rooms. The many leather couches were so plumply upholstered as to make it more likely that they would throw one off than welcome one in. It was a household run by a woman on a perpetual diet of the senses. It would be uncharitable of me to suggest a likeness between Honor and Janice Tovey – suffice it to say that I understood at once why Timothy Tovey should have sought solace in Gabriella's arms.

Mrs Tovey being out at a fund-raising, I could not pass on Gabriella's message to her in person – somewhat, I must say, to my relief. I was shown instead into the library, where I found Timothy Tovey, a courteous white-haired man who still had about him the remnants of the vigorous good looks of his youth. I had, I think, expected to see him bowed down by grief at the loss of Gabriella, but he seemed cheerful enough, even lively. He was obviously a man with a great appetite for life. He talked to me freely; he was a member of the GNFR and although I am not of the high priesthood I am sufficiently advanced in the lay hierarchy to hear confession, or, as we like to call it, life-story.

'What, my Gabriella!' he exclaimed. 'Taped by the priests! Come back as a re-wind! Well, it doesn't surprise me. That woman's egocentricity would survive a hundred deaths. Waiting for me in the hereafter? Janice isn't going to like that! Waiting for Janice, too, you say? Oh, my Lord!' And he laughed, heartily.

I was, I must say, a little taken aback. He apologised. 'I loved Gabriella,' he said, 'very much indeed at one time of my life. But is there to be no end to love? I held her hand when she died simply because she had sent for me, quite out of the blue. I had not seen her or spoken to her for twenty years: though GSWITS knows she had cost me enough in that time. And, seeing her as she was, old and ill, on her deathbed, it was hard to remember just why she had inspired such passion in me. She could be a very trying woman, you know. She once refused to see me for two years, on the grounds that she had discovered I slept with my own wife in a double bed!'

'Three,' I said. I tried not to sound too reproachful. Timothy Tovey had his part to play. As do we all.

'As long as that? I can hardly remember. But I do recall she wanted to run off with some Greek waiter: she spent two years trying to persuade him to marry her, but she failed and came back to me. That was what all that was about. Did she tell you the truth? I doubt it. I first encountered her via her dental X-rays. We shared the same dentist, way back, when I was young. The poor man was obviously hopelessly in love with her — quite deranged. *"See,"* I remember him saying, waving the X-ray plates of a total stranger in front of me, as I reclined helpless in his chair, *"a perfect arch! A crime if anything happens to those teeth."* I could not help but notice the name. Gabriella Sumpter! It entranced me, together with the concept of a perfect arch. And I suppose it is in a man's nature to love and want what another man loves and wants, albeit a dentist. So I sought out the young woman, and found the most beautiful creature imaginable, living with, though not married to, a prosperous, fashionable and very boring young doctor. I resolved at once to make her my mistress.'

And so the sorry story continued. Timothy Tovey had no intention of damaging his prospects in the diplomatic service by marrying Gabriella, though he confessed to promising her he would, the more easily to seduce the poor woman. They succeeded in keeping their relationship hidden from the doctor for some years, until Miss Martock, then resident as housekeeper in Orme Square, eventually became party to it — and she it was who, under a terrible burden of guilt, informed Aldred Ray about what was going on under the pear tree at home, and in a little service flat in Mayfair away from home. Gabriella forgave Miss Martock for her indiscretion — she relied heavily by then upon her housekeeper's dressmaking skills. But Aldred could not forgive Gabriella; alas, he hanged himself in the bathroom, there where little pink-lacquered birds flew across gilded tiles. After which scandal, of course, it was all the more difficult for Timothy Tovey to regularise his relationship with Gabriella, although he did admit that at this stage he very much wanted to. He introduced Gabriella to his mother, and to his surprise Lady Julia quite liked the girl, in spite of her past, and would almost, he thought, have consented to the match, and encouraged him to face and overcome any consequent difficulties in his career, had it not been for Gabriella's extraordinary behaviour, one morning, over the spoiling in the wash of a cheap muslin nightgown. She had fussed and carried on as if it had been some expensive silk extravaganza, quite spoiling Lady Julia's breakfast. It was apparent that the girl had no idea at all how to manage the servants. She had been badly brought up. A diplomat's wife has to know how to deal with staff. It is the key to her husband's success.

And so, thoughts of marriage were abandoned and Gabriella was set up by Lady Julia in the little house in St John's Wood, where it seemed she could do no harm. Here, Timothy Tovey explained, he was a frequent visitor, until shortage of money obliged him to marry Janice — a less distant relative of royalty — who was able to both line his pocket and further his career.

'I loved Janice,' Timothy Tovey said to me, 'as a man loves a wife, and I appreciated Gabriella as a man appreciates a mistress. The wife stokes the fire; the mistress warms her hands at the blaze.' The passion between himself and Gabriella had gradually faded. Some ten years into the marriage, when Janice had put him on a diet, came a time when the flame rekindled, and Timothy Tovey visited Gabriella more frequently than the once-a-fortnight which had been his custom. But that too soon passed. The bedclothes, he complained, were always uncomfortably scratchy. Finally the visits stopped altogether.

Children? They had never discussed the matter. It would have been totally inappropriate for Gabriella to have had his, Timothy Tovey's, offspring. He could not have acknowledged them. Nor, he thought, would he have continued to support Gabriella had she had children by another man. As it was, he believed he had dealt very fairly with her. But still sometimes, just sometimes, he would wake up in the night, and reach out for Gabriella, and find instead the staunch body of Janice.

'And you feel like weeping,' I finished his sentence for him, since he could not, 'but quite what for you can't make out.'

We were interrupted by the arrival of Janice Tovey, and I was not sorry. He seemed to be telling me a tale of waste and sorrow: of lives and happiness thrown away. But Janice, although I must say plain of feature, was a determined and positive woman, who seemed to have lived a good enough life, and when warned by her husband that Gabriella was roaming the city as a re-wind merely laughed and said: 'She never bothered me when she was alive. Why should she now she's a ghost?' Poor Gabriella, I thought. The only one in the world to take herself seriously — but that, no doubt, is the fate of women who do not marry, and who do not have children, for whatever reason.

'Love', I said reflectively to Honor, when I got home, 'is a woman's whole existence. To men, it is a thing apart.' Honor just laughed, and put a plate of high-fibre beans on unbuttered whole meal toast in front of me, and said I had changed, probably for the better, but I must now stop thinking about love and get on with the reform of the GNFR. Honor is, of course, quite right. Strange days, indeed. Oh, strange days.